the head is dead

Tanya Landman is the author of many books for children, including *Waking Merlin* and *Merlin's Apprentice*, *The World's Bellybutton* and *The Kraken Snores*, and three stories featuring the characters Flotsam and Jetsam. Of *The Head is Dead* Tanya says, "An advert for a murder mystery evening at a local school caught my attention. I started to wonder if there were tensions and rivalries in the staff room. Suppose the whole event was a plot to divert attention from a real murder?"

Tanya is also the author of two novels for teenagers: *Apache*, which was shortlisted for the Carnegie Medal and the Booktrust Teenage Fiction Prize, and *The Goldsmith's Daughter*, which was nominated for the Guardian Children's Fiction Prize. Since 1992, Tanya has also been part of Storybox Theatre. She lives with her family in Devon.

You can find out more about Tanya Landman
and her books by visiting her website at
www.tanyalandman.com

the head is dead

tanya landman

WALKER
BOOKS

First published in Great Britain 2009 by Walker Books Ltd
87 Vauxhall Walk, London SE11 5HJ

2 4 6 8 10 9 7 5 3 1

Text © 2009 Tanya Landman

This book has been typeset in Slimbach

Printed and bound in Great Britain by Clays Ltd, St Ives plc

British Library Cataloguing in Publication Data:
a catalogue record for this book is
available from the British Library

ISBN 978-1-4063-1463-2

www.walker.co.uk

For Mum — who enjoys a good
murder as much as I do

It *was her mother's fault. Of course it was! She understood that now. He'd explained it all to her very carefully. If only the stupid woman hadn't written her will like that. If only it hadn't involved quite so much money!*

But she had, and now there was no choice.

They had to get him away.

Tonight. While there was still somewhere to hide him.

Weeping softly, she kissed his cold forehead and stroked his cheek for the last time. Whispering goodbye, she tenderly wrapped the quilt around him before pulling it up over his face.

In the silent darkness they carried him out of his bedroom and away to where he could be safe and at peace. When the job was done, they returned to the house, shutting the door behind them just as the first blackbird's song pierced the stillness.

It was dawn. The sun was rising. Everything would be fine now. He'd promised that in the morning all their problems would be solved – and she'd believed him. He had to be right. He always was. Wasn't he?

easter bunnies

My name is Poppy Fields. I'm quite a peaceful sort of person really: I don't believe in violence. So let me say right here and now that it wasn't my idea to kill the head.

It was the deputy I wanted to murder.

Not in real life, you understand. The whole event was supposed to be a bit of light entertainment – a fun way of getting people to part with their cash. We never expected anyone to actually die.

It happened at Easter, which for some strange reason was almost slap-bang in the middle of March. My friend Graham did his best to explain it to me, going on about Gregorian and lunisolar calendars and paschal full moons, but I still didn't get why it was so early. I mean, Christmas is always on 25 December; New Year's Day is always on 1 January; my birthday's always on 7 August. Why does Easter have to move around all over the place? And I wasn't the only one who was confused by it. While the schools in our county took their two weeks off right after the egg-based-festival weekend, everybody else was having their holiday in April. Which meant that when my mum, Lili, got offered a job in Barnford transforming the St Andrew's Primary School car park into a wildlife haven just after Easter, she had to take me along with her.

It was a five-hour drive from where we live, so the school secretary, Mrs Plumtree, had booked us into a local bed and breakfast. Graham came too because his mother was busy at work with some big event and she reckoned that if he was with us, he wouldn't spend his whole holiday glued to his computer.

When we arrived in Barnford, the lady who ran the B&B, Mrs Oates ("call me Marjorie"), filled us in on the school's background before we'd even unpacked our bags.

"The head, Mrs King, hasn't been there long," Marjorie said. "St Andrew's wasn't doing too well in the league tables under the old chap. He had a mild heart attack or a stroke or something over Christmas, so he retired on health grounds and the governors brought in Mrs King. They said they wanted a 'new broom'. She's made quite an impact already."

Marjorie slapped a copy of the local paper down on the table. Mrs King was there on the front page staring aggressively at the camera under a headline screaming: HEAD CUTS OUT DEAD WOOD.

Mum read the article out loud. There was all sorts of stuff about how Mrs King was going to "shake things up" and "knock the place into shape" and that sometimes you had to "be cruel to be kind". She'd promised that "sub-standard teaching will not be tolerated" and that "poor pupil behaviour will be rigorously dealt with". "I'm not afraid of permanently excluding children who prove disruptive," she'd declared.

Mum handed the newspaper back and said, "Phew! That all sounds a bit menacing. I bet the staff are terrified, aren't they?"

"Not to mention the kids," I added. It seemed to me that Mrs King really knew how to make enemies.

"I wouldn't know," said Marjorie, pursing her lips with evident relish. "I suppose you'll find out soon enough."

* * *

Mum's meeting with Mrs King was scheduled for 9.15 sharp the next morning.

Mum didn't want to be late on her first day, not if Mrs King was as scary as she sounded in the paper. We arrived early, and I took the opportunity to observe the staff while we sat in the reception area. I'm dead interested in other people – studying the intricate details of human behaviour is a hobby of mine – and this particular group of subjects was especially fascinating. They all looked slightly stunned: like the survivors of a violent earthquake who have crawled out from the rubble of a collapsed building and are temporarily dazzled by the sun and confused by the changed landscape. They were treading carefully as though cracks might open in the ground beneath their feet.

The only person who seemed unaffected was Mrs Plumtree. She was a smiling, jolly woman with a massive, matronly bosom and she exuded waves of sweet-smelling floral perfume.

"Hello, dear," she said to Mum. "How lovely to meet you at last! How's the B&B? Was it comfortable? Did you sleep all right?"

The reception area was really an oversized porch at the front of the building. The secretary's office was on the right, a sliding window granting access to people who wanted to buy lunch tickets or hand in lost property. Mrs Plumtree kept it open so she could chat while Mum waited for her meeting.

"You'll find that the staff are all a little tense," she told Mum in a confidential manner. "Mrs King's really upset one or two people, including the governors. I'm afraid Mr Edwards – the chairman – isn't too keen on the environmental project. The car park was only constructed two years ago and he feels it's rather a waste of resources. But Mrs King likes to do things her own way and it's not proving too popular. Of course it's no problem for me, I'm retiring at the end of the year."

"Really?" said Mum. "You don't look old enough."

Mrs Plumtree laughed. "Bless you, dear, that's very sweet! Actually, I'm taking early retirement. Ricky, my son, has special needs, you see. I've decided to spend more time with him."

Mum asked, "Is that Ricky?" She was pointing to a vast collection of photographs that were stuck on the wall next to Mrs Plumtree's computer. They all featured the same brilliantly blue-eyed young man in various exotic locations: smiling in front of the pyramids, grinning by the Eiffel Tower, waving from the top of the Empire State Building.

"No, that's Davy, Ricky's twin. He's in Peru at the moment." She waved a photo of him standing in the ruins of Machu Picchu. "He sent me this just last week."

"That must cost a bit!" said Mum. "He must work very hard in between trips to afford it all."

Mrs Plumtree flushed slightly. "Actually, I pay for them, dear," she said. "I don't begrudge him. He so loves to travel." She heaved a sigh so deep that her bosom quivered like a plate of jelly. "It's strange how life turns out, isn't it? They were born a few minutes apart, that's all. But Ricky had the umbilical cord wrapped around his neck, so he was deprived of oxygen at birth. It caused brain damage. So Ricky stays at home, and Davy goes all over the world. We really don't see much of him any more."

"That's hard on you," said Mum sympathetically.

"Oh no, dear. I miss him, of course. I miss him so badly!" She dabbed at the corners of her eyes with a tissue before making a visible effort to pull herself together. "Really, I musn't grumble. It's not like the awful things some people have to cope with. We have a roof over our heads, and we're healthy and well fed. That's more than you can say for lots of people in the world, isn't it?"

The clock ticked around towards 9.15, but at 9.12 precisely a large man with a scary-looking set of tattoos down his arms came crashing through the front door dragging a kid behind him, and – without knocking – burst into Mrs King's office.

Mrs Plumtree paled. "Oh dear," she said. "That's Mr Walters. I wonder what he wants?" She didn't have to say any more, because we could hear the drama from beginning to end.

"What's this rubbish about Craig swearing?" demanded Mr Walters.

"Your son used foul and offensive language in front of my secretary yesterday, Mr Walters," came back a crisp, clear voice that I took to be Mrs King's. "As you know, we have a zero-tolerance approach to swearing at this school. He will be excluded from attending until I can be sure he's learnt to control his tongue."

"He says he didn't do it," Mr Walters growled menacingly.

"I didn't do nothing," chipped in a kid's voice. "Honest, miss."

"You *didn't do nothing*," echoed Mrs King witheringly. "Let me see. Would that be like the time you didn't flush Billy Kane's pencil case down the toilet? Or the time you didn't throw Willa Smith's shoes over the fence?"

Craig didn't answer.

"He says he didn't do it and I believe him," said his father.

"That's all very well, Mr Walters, but I don't."

"You've got no right to send him home!" roared Craig's dad.

"I have every right, Mr Walters. I'm the head." Her words shot out like bullets. "Until your son can speak without turning the air around him blue; until he learns to admit when he has done wrong; until he learns to face the consequences of his actions, he will remain excluded."

"I can make you take him back, you know. I'll go to the governors. I can force you."

"Over my dead body," growled Mrs King.

Her office door was flung open with such gusto that we all jumped a few centimetres in the air. Mr Walters stormed back out, dragging the foul-mouthed Craig behind him. Then Mrs King appeared, calm and unruffled, in the doorway.

"Ms Fields," she said, shaking Mum energetically by the hand. "Do come in. Let's get started."

Graham and I had planned to just wait in the reception area until they'd finished their meeting, but Mrs King was like a force of nature – she swept us up and the next thing we knew we were sitting meekly in her office listening to her plans.

"I want the entire car park to go. People will have to walk to school in future. Think of the benefits: it will be good for their health and good for the planet.

There are no losers with this project."

She wanted a pond for newts and a nettle patch for butterflies, a log pile for hedgehogs and berry bushes for the birds.

"I was at Cornborough Primary for a meeting last term," she told Mum. "I gather you did the environmental area there?"

Mum nodded. "Yes. It was a few years ago now."

"Well, what I've got in mind is something like that, only twice as big. The sooner we can get started, the better. We've got most of the money we need in the school fund and we're having a spring fayre this Sunday to raise the rest. If you draw the plans up this week you can start digging on Monday."

She swung around in her swivelly chair and fixed me and Graham with a steely stare. "What are you two going to do while your mother's working?" she demanded. "I hope you have something constructive in mind. I can't bear idleness."

Of course we hadn't planned anything other than hanging around in the park and watching telly at the B&B – we were on holiday after all. But that didn't seem to be the kind of answer you could give to someone like Mrs King. Words popped out of my mouth that had bypassed my brain completely.

"We could help with the fayre," I offered.

"Excellent idea!" barked Mrs King. "Let's see… We already have an egg hunt for the infants. I know Easter Sunday was last weekend, but one of the dads has offered to dress up as a bunny, so I don't suppose anyone will mind. We've got all the usual stalls and sideshows covered. But one of my teachers – Mr Piper, I think – came up with the novel idea of a murder mystery trail for the older children and grown-ups to enjoy. Sadly nobody's had time to do anything about it until now. Think you could arrange one?"

"Yes," Graham said helplessly. He blinked in surprise. Clearly he was experiencing the same problem as me.

"Now I know what vivid imaginations children have, so I want you to come up with a plot." Mrs King was going full-steam ahead. "The more outrageous it is, the better. A body… A series of clues… Everyone has to pay to enter, of course. People who come up with the right answer will have their names put in a hat. The first one pulled out wins the prize. Got that? Good. I'll expect some ideas on my desk in the morning. Off you go."

So that was that. While Mum measured the car park and began to draw up a plan of the area, we started work on a project of our own.

the grand plan

Planning the whole thing was fun. I mean, Graham and I knew a lot about real-life murders, so it was quite nice to be making one up. Or at least it was to begin with.

We sat in the school library and worked out a stupidly complicated plot. The victim was a nuclear scientist masquerading as a teacher who was secretly married to a woman in Russia but dating a local nurse who was really an undercover spy who was in love with a gardener who had a brother who was violently opposed to nuclear power and determined to stop the scientist designing a new reactor. You get the picture. There'd be objects littered around the place – a jar labelled

URANIUM, a syringe, a wedding ring and a Russian passport. Each one would have a written clue attached that would lead to the next one until finally you discovered the body and had to work out who'd done it and why. Our victim was going to be squashed flat by the blade of a wind turbine – a good, symbolic end.

"What do we do if it rains?" Graham asked.

"Rain?" I said, incredulous. "On Mrs King's spring fayre? It wouldn't dare."

We were going to use a dummy for the dead body, but then a teacher called Mr Stuart told us that Mrs King was very keen on using a real person "to add an authentic touch". So we decided that Mr Piper – the deputy head, who'd come up with the idea of the trail – could be the victim. If anyone was willing to lie motionless all afternoon covered in tomato sauce, it was bound to be him. But just before the bell went, Miss Maris, the librarian, came in.

"You're working on Mr Stuart's scheme, aren't you?" she asked.

"The murder trail?" I said. "I thought it was Mr Piper's idea."

"Was it?" She looked puzzled. "Oh well." She bent over to look at what we'd done. "Are you sure you want Mr Piper to be the corpse?"

"Yes," Graham said.

"Only I just heard in the staff room that Mrs King's keen to do it." She pulled a face. We all did. The thought of not doing what Mrs King wanted was too terrible to contemplate. So we changed things around and made her the victim instead.

Next morning, while Mum was sketching a proposed layout, we took our plans to Mrs King. She seemed really pleased. She actually patted us both on the back, which was kind of like being walloped by a charging rhinoceros, but neither of us complained. We couldn't. She'd knocked the air clean out of our lungs and we were gasping for breath. It was only then that she noticed we'd given her the part of the corpse, and I have to say that she didn't seem too pleased about it.

"I suppose I have to show willing," she said brusquely. "It's what leadership is all about. And it's better than having wet sponges thrown at me."

Neither of us were capable of speech at that point, so we didn't say anything. She assigned us the task of carrying out the plan – getting the props, writing the clues, working out where they were going to be hidden, that kind of thing – and we went off without a word.

Organizing the details of the trail should have been simple. Mrs Plumtree showed us a whole cupboard full of stuff left over from school plays and assemblies that we could use. But by the end of the day everything had completely changed.

It was weird. Teachers kept coming up to us and giving us bits of advice or telling us things that had been said in the staff room. Bit by bit, line by line, the whole plan got altered so that what we ended up with wasn't anything like what Graham and I had originally thought up.

OK, so Mrs King was still the victim. But she wasn't going to be dead in the shed at the corner of the football pitch, like we'd wanted. She told us she'd been advised that health and safety wouldn't allow it, and Mr Stuart said he'd overheard Mrs King say that it might frighten any little kids who were doing the Easter egg hunt if they saw her by accident. So we thought we'd stick her in the mobile classroom on the playground, but the caretaker said he'd been told that all the classrooms would be out of bounds for the fayre. Everywhere else we suggested seemed to already be taken for one activity or another. Eventually Mr Piper told us he'd heard it was OK to use the narrow path behind the kitchen. There was a steep bank opposite that led up to the field, but it was so overgrown with bushes that she'd be well hidden.

We thought we'd finally got it sorted, but then

we were told that tomato sauce was out because it might attract flies (according to Miss Maris), or wasps (according to Mr Stuart). And Mr Piper said that being squished by a wind turbine blade was a bad idea because it might give people nightmares. We thought of strangling her with a bit of rope, but apparently Mrs King objected to that on the grounds of taste. We invented all manner of different ways of finishing her off, but one by one we had to abandon them. In the end the only thing no one objected to was knocking her out with sleeping pills and suffocating her with a cushion. It didn't have the dramatic appeal of the ketchup, but none of the teachers complained.

Then – just when it was all arranged – the issue of timing came up. We'd thought we'd hand out the first clues as soon as the fayre began, but Mrs King said that Miss Maris was worried it would take attention away from the other activities, so Mr Stuart suggested that we start an hour later. Mr Piper said it would give Mrs King the chance to open the fayre before taking up her position as the body on the path. So we put that down on the plan and waited with bated breath to see if anyone would tell us we couldn't do it. When none of the teachers sidled up with helpful remarks, staff room rumours or grim comments, Graham and I breathed a sigh of relief.

Later on, Mum bought fish and chips and we ate them in front of the B&B's telly. We were watching a gardening programme about some big country estate and there was a shot of sheep being herded into a pen by a black-and-white dog. I suddenly said, "I know exactly how they feel."

"What?" Mum was baffled.

But Graham put his plate down on the floor and turned to me. "I know what you mean," he said seriously.

"It's like we're a couple of sheep who've been herded by an invisible sheepdog, isn't it? We've been steered every step of the way…"

We looked back at the TV. As we watched, the farmer closed the gate with a clang. The sheep were trapped.

"An invisible sheepdog…" Graham echoed.

And then we both turned to each other and said, "I wonder who it is?"

staff meeting

Graham and I were both jumpy on the day of the spring fayre, because of that weird suspicion that our murder trail had been controlled by someone. So many different teachers had made so many different remarks and yet we had the feeling that one person had steered and directed everyone, including us. What we couldn't work out was who and why. It was sinister enough to make us feel very uneasy.

Mum stayed back at the B&B to put the finishing touches to her design. The school was only round the corner, so Graham and I walked there two hours before the fayre was due to open. We needed to lay out the clues and sort out a table with pens and paper for people taking part. We also wanted to get a stack of coins from Mrs Plumtree in case anyone needed change. But before we could do any of that, we had to go to a meeting in the hall with everyone else involved. All the teachers were there, along with various mums and dads.

Mrs King had a megaphone and was clearly planning to use it. She dumped her handbag on a table at the back of the hall and then marched to the front to address her troops. Standing on the stage she looked like a character from an old war film – a general before the start of a Very Important Battle – and I mentioned it to Graham.

"She does bear a striking resemblance to Winston Churchill," he replied.

"Let's hope she doesn't ask us to lay down our lives for our country," I joked. Which wasn't very funny really, given what happened later.

All the staff had really entered into the spirit of the thing. Mr Stuart was wearing an old pair of jeans and a faded sweatshirt. He'd volunteered to have wet sponges thrown at him, so he was dressed for the job. Then there was Mr Piper, who was running the coconut shy, and Miss Maris, who was doing the lucky dip and the tombola. The chair of governors, Mr Edwards, had arranged a football event – Beat the Goalie. Quite honestly, he was so large that he'd only have to stand in the centre of the goal and nothing would get past him. One mum was doing Pin the Tail on the Donkey, a dad was organizing three-legged races and someone's big sister was doing face painting. The Easter bunny was dressed, armed with a basket of eggs and ready to hop. Everyone was present and correct and poised for action. Everyone apart from Mrs Plumtree, who was supposed to be running the raffle. When Mrs King called her name and there was no answer, her brow furrowed into a dangerous series of creases.

"She's gone AWOL," murmured Graham.

"What?" I whispered.

"Absent Without Leave," he hissed back, flashing me one of his blink-and-you-miss-it grins.

"Oh, I see. I guess she'll be first up for the firing squad, then," I said.

Mrs King began to hand out bags of small change to the stall holders. Graham and I joined the queue. When Mrs King handed Mr Piper his money, she said something to him about making himself useful and earning his keep. His face flickered with an emotion I couldn't quite identify. I had the weirdest sensation. All of a sudden I could smell malice in the air. It was as strong as the scent of hot dogs at a fairground. Invisible, but very definitely there.

"Did you hear what Mrs King said to Mr Piper?" I asked Graham quietly.

"Yes. I think it was meant to be a joke."

Just then there was a commotion behind us and Mrs Plumtree burst into the hall. The reason for her lateness was obvious immediately. She had Ricky with her.

"So sorry," she said, red-faced and breathless. "Ricky's carer was supposed to be looking after him, but she's gone down with that horrible bug that's been going round. I couldn't leave him at home on his own."

"Of course not," said Mrs King briskly. She glanced sympathetically at Ricky, but he didn't meet her eyes. He looked as though he didn't like making eye contact with anyone. Instead he wrapped his arms around himself and started to rock backwards and forwards, humming softly and staring dreamily into space.

With Ricky there, Mrs Plumtree couldn't do the raffle outside where the rest of us would be.

"He doesn't really like being out in unfamiliar places," she said. "And big crowds sometimes upset him. Suppose I have him in the office with me? Everyone will have to walk past it to get to the field, so I'll be in the perfect position. I can sell the raffle tickets from there."

Mrs King agreed immediately, so Mrs Plumtree gently led Ricky away to settle him down in her office. Just before we went out to set things up, Mrs Plumtree emerged and thoughtfully pressed a jug of orange squash into Graham's hands.

"You'll be needing that, dears," she said kindly. "Take it from me, it'll be a long, thirsty afternoon."

At two o'clock the fayre opened. Graham and I had no idea what might be about to happen, but we felt strangely tense. All afternoon we both kept one eye on the clock and one eye on the grown-ups.

Thrusting her bag at Mr Piper for safekeeping, Mrs King did her big welcoming speech, urging everyone to dig deep into their pockets for the sake of their health and that of the planet. Then we were off. Or at least everyone else was. Graham and I had been strictly forbidden to get our bit going before 3 p.m. so we wandered around throwing balls at coconuts, sticking our arms into barrels of sawdust to pull out plastic prizes and watching everyone very closely for signs of odd behaviour.

At precisely 2.45, Mrs King – with a slightly irritated glance in our direction – went off to get changed into her nuclear scientist outfit.

At 2.50 I was suddenly desperate for the toilet. The

nearest one was the staff loo right next to Mrs King's office. As helpers on the day, we'd been given special permission to use it, so I nipped in and had what my mum would have called a "nasty upset stomach" and I called a "bad case of the squits". It was totally embarrassing, because when I came out Mrs King was standing at the sink and I realized she must have heard everything. I blushed scarlet.

She was shoving some pills down her throat. "Headache," she said, looking at me in the mirror. "These events always get to me. And I can't say the prospect of being a corpse all afternoon has helped." She sniffed the pongy air pointedly and remarked, "I see the tension's getting to you too. Are you all set?"

"Yes," I said, fighting the urge to salute. "We're just about to start."

"Good. See you later, then."

I was perplexed. "Mrs King still doesn't seem pleased about being the body," I told Graham when I got back. "She acted like we'd forced her into it."

"I thought that's what she wanted," said Graham, looking mystified. "That's what Miss Maris said, wasn't it?"

We couldn't talk about it any more, because at 2.57 the stress got to Graham too and he dashed off to the toilet, leaving me alone on our stall just as Mr Edwards announced over the loudspeaker that we were ready for business.

I was anxious for a second, but fortunately there wasn't exactly a rush for the first clue. For about five minutes nothing much happened. Graham eventually came back and we stood there shuffling awkwardly from one foot to the other. Then a couple of kids ambled over, paid their cash and took a piece of paper and a pencil. A few more followed, and then one or two parents took up the challenge. By 3.30, twenty-seven people were roaming about the field looking for clues.

It was taking them a long time to go from one clue to the other. "Do you think we've made it too compli-cated?" I said, worried.

"No," said Graham. "It's scientifically proven that the more you challenge your brain, the more you increase your capacity for logical thought. We're doing them a favour."

At 3.55 Mr Piper ran out of coconuts and had to go to the supermarket to get some more. Mr Edwards decided he'd been hit in the stomach by a football once too often during Beat the Goalie and took a break. He ambled over to us and picked up the first clue.

"I'll have a shot at this," he said. Handing Graham his money, he set off across the field.

There was nothing much for me and Graham to

do, so we finished the orange squash. We were both jiggling around uncomfortably with sore bottoms, cramping stomachs and a dreadful feeling of unease that neither of us could understand or explain away. At 4.05 Graham ran to the toilet again and Miss Maris went to fetch herself a cup of tea.

It was then that I spotted Mr Walters – dad of the excluded Craig – standing on the far side of the field as if he was looking for someone. He suddenly reached inside his jacket to pull out his mobile phone. After that, he started pushing his way through the crowds, heading slowly towards the school. My vague sense of anxiety sharpened. There's trouble, I thought fretfully. I wonder what he's up to?

Graham returned, looking slightly green.

"Mr Walters is over there," I told him. "Do you think he's looking for Mrs King?"

"Might be," Graham replied. "She could probably do with a visitor. Mrs Plumtree just asked me to take her a cup of tea. She must be bored stiff – she was yawning her head off. She could hardly keep her eyes open. No one's even close to finding her. I read some research recently that suggested boredom can be more difficult to endure than physical pain."

Mr Walters disappeared from view and our attention was taken up by a sudden yell that came from the direction of the office, making us both jump.

"What was that?" I asked.

"Ricky was getting upset when I went to the loo," Graham said. "There's too much noise or something. Mrs Plumtree said he doesn't like crowds, didn't she?"

"I know how he feels," I replied. "Something's not right."

"Quite. I wish we knew what it was. Anyway… She was trying to calm him down."

But whatever Mrs Plumtree was doing to Ricky wasn't working. We could hear the sounds of his distress quite clearly from our stall, and it added to the awful sensation of impending doom that was hanging over both of us.

At 4.12 Mr Stuart, who was now soaked to the skin, decided to change into some dry clothes to avoid getting hypothermia and disappeared into the school. Mr Piper returned from the supermarket laden with coconuts and Miss Maris came back to the tombola with a steaming cup of tea. Everyone else seemed perfectly cheerful. A bit too cheerful, if anything. Were the teachers' smiles a shade too bright? Were their jokes a fraction too loud and hearty? The sun was shining and it was a beautiful spring day. Everything appeared to be perfectly normal. And yet there was Graham, biting his nails and fidgeting, and me, unable to stand still for longer than a second – both of us acting like we expected disaster to strike at any moment.

By 4.17 Mr Stuart was back on the stall in dry clothes ready to be drenched again, and it was my turn to sprint for the toilet for another round of Exploding Bottom. Ricky was still upset. I could hear him crying, and in between his sobs I could pick out Mrs Plumtree's soothing voice. After I'd finished in the toilet, I went past the office again and Mrs Plumtree poked her head out through the door, looking flushed.

"Are you OK?" I asked. "I mean, is Ricky all right?"

"He'll be fine," she said, her voice a little wobbly. "Poor love! It's the noise of the loudspeaker that's getting to him. If I'd thought about it, I'd have kept him at home, but I didn't want to let everyone down. Still, I've given him his medication now, so that will sort him out." Sure enough, the heartbreaking sounds of Ricky's distress were beginning to soften and fade, and for a second I felt my own tension ease slightly.

But then Mrs Plumtree said, "Could you take these to Mrs King? I forgot to give them to Graham earlier." She handed me a plate with a couple of chocolate biscuits on it.

"Sure," I said. I took it and went down the corridor, past the staff room, across the hall and through the kitchen, the sounds of the fayre echoing eerily in the empty building.

I opened the door to the outside world and suddenly that vague feeling of unease became as solid as a brick wall. I could see in an instant that something was horribly, disastrously wrong.

Mrs King was lying on the path exactly where she was supposed to be, flat on her back with a red silk cushion over her face. She was perfectly still; way too still for a living person.

And she wasn't alone.

Mr Walters was kneeling beside her. And his hand was pressing down on the cushion he'd used to suffocate her.

the head is dead

Mr Walters stared at me for a second, his mouth hanging open. He looked as shocked as I felt.

"She phoned me," he said in a confused little whisper. "How could she phone me? She's dead!"

Then he looked at Mrs King again and seemed to realize he'd been Caught in the Act. Staggering to his feet, he ran off before I could even try to stop him. He was still clutching the cushion.

Mrs King's face was a horrible colour. Her lips were pale lilac; her cheeks a blotchy purple. It was a truly gruesome sight.

I called her name. I even prodded her, although I knew it was too late. I've seen enough bodies to know when someone's had it. She didn't move a muscle.

And then – before I'd had a chance to do anything – Mr Edwards came slithering down the slope between the bushes, shouting a triumphant "Aha! Found the corpse! Am I the first?"

"She's dead," I told him.

"I know," he said eagerly, helping himself to a chocolate biscuit from the plate I was still holding. "Murdered with a combination of sleeping pills and suffocation. And I've worked out the culprit!"

"No," I said firmly.

"I have!" he protested. "It was the gardener, wasn't it? In a fit of jealous rage?"

"Well, yes, but…"

"There you are, then. Aren't you going to congratulate me, Mrs King?"

She didn't stir.

"Mrs King?" he repeated, a little uncertainly.

"She's really dead," I explained. "Not acting. She's been murdered."

I don't think I've ever seen a grown-up's face collapse as completely as Mr Edwards' did then. It sort of sank like a badly made cake and he gasped, "No! It's not possible! Not on school premises." His hand went to his chest as if he was about to have a heart attack. And then he said, aghast, "Whatever will the papers say?"

What they said was that it was an open-and-shut case. I mean, we'd heard Mr Walters complaining about Craig's exclusion. It turned out that he already had a criminal record involving a fist fight in a pub on New Year's Eve. And I'd seen him right there holding the cushion over Mrs King's face. Evidence didn't come clearer than that. They arrested him within the hour. He'd gone straight home and was making a cup of tea, the cushion still stuffed under one arm, when they picked him up.

I was the key witness. Graham and I spent the rest of the day at the police station giving our statements. Mum had to come along too, to be the Responsible Adult present. It was just as well we'd paid so much attention to what was going on that afternoon, because we pretty much knew the sequence of events. But the interview kept being interrupted because we both had to dash to the toilet every few minutes. It was mortifying, and I didn't understand why it was happening. Detective Chief Inspector Swan – the woman in charge of the investigation – thought it must be nerves. Mum put it down to last night's fish and chips, although she seemed OK.

We tried to stick to the facts – we knew from experience that the police aren't always keen to hear theories from kids – but we couldn't help mentioning how we'd been steered into using ideas that weren't our own. Yet the more we tried to explain, the lamer it sounded. DCI Swan said, "Do you have any proof of this?"

"No," we told her. "It's just a feeling."

"A feeling?" she repeated, one eyebrow raised.

"Yes," we chorused firmly.

By the end of the interview she was looking at us as though we were certifiably insane. "You're going round and round in circles, kids," she said. "But you're not heading anywhere. Just like two hamsters in a wheel."

It wasn't the kindest comment anyone's ever made about me and Graham, but maybe she was right, because when I woke up in the middle of the night I started to question what I'd actually seen. I'd been dreaming about Mr Walters, frozen and motionless, next to Mrs King.

OK, so he had a criminal record. But, I thought, taking a swing at someone in a pub on New Year's Eve is a different thing altogether from a cold-blooded murder in broad daylight, isn't it?

He'd had his hand on the cushion, true enough. It *looked* like he'd been pressing it down, but I'd only seen him for a moment before he ran away. What if it had already been there on her face? Suppose he'd been about to lift it off her? Would I have spotted the difference? And why had his mouth been open like that? Why was he so shocked?

According to DCI Swan, Mr Walters had sworn blind that Mrs King was dead when he got there. That he was bending down to see who the prostrate figure was.

"Well, he would say that, wouldn't he?" Graham said at breakfast the next day. Mum was in the shower and Marjorie was in the kitchen frying bacon, so it was safe to talk. "It's a well-known fact that some murderers go through a period of denial right after they commit a crime. It doesn't matter how compellingly the facts are stacked against them: it's as if they can't accept what they've done. They block it out. Pretend it hasn't happened. It's a recognized psychological phenomenon."

"All right," I replied. "But think about it for a second. What if Mr Walters is telling the truth? What if she was already dead?"

"If that's true, it must have happened just minutes before he got there. She was killed between 4.05 – when I took her a cup of tea – and 4.20, when you found her. It can't have been before 4.05, because she was fine when I saw her."

I thought back for a moment. "Hang on, though, Graham. She wasn't fine. You said she was yawning her head off."

"She was bored."

"Really?" My palms started to tingle. I had the sudden feeling that I was on to something. "Are you sure?"

"What else would make her yawn?"

"Think of the murder trail, Graham! What knocked out the nuclear scientist? Sleeping pills!"

There was a long pause. I could practically hear the cogs in Graham's brain crunching together. "Do you mean you think she might have been drugged?"

I nodded. There was a long, thoughtful pause.

"It would be extremely uncanny if that were the case," Graham said finally.

"True," I said. "But it fits, doesn't it? We knew we were being steered, and now we know why – someone used us to kill Mrs King. And I don't think it was Mr Walters. I reckon he's as innocent as we are."

"Another sheep, then," said Graham. "It seems the flock is growing."

There was only one answer to that. "*Baaaaaa*."

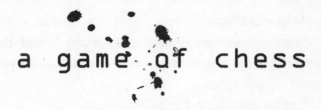

a game of chess

When it came to suspects, we were spoilt for choice. Mrs King hadn't been at the school for long but she'd already made a whole bunch of enemies. According to what Mrs Plumtree had told Mum, everyone was worried for one reason or another. The staff were worried about their jobs, parents were worried about their kids being excluded and the governors were worried because she didn't consult them about stuff.

But which of them hated her enough to kill her? And which of them was clever enough to organize a plot involving such a complicated series of manoeuvres?

"It's like a game of chess," Graham said.

"Is it?" I don't play chess, so I wasn't quite sure what he was on about.

"Yes… A vast and complex strategy with each move planned way ahead. We're up against someone very clever. A person who can plan logically and methodically, and who possesses a remarkably devious and cunning mind."

The thought wasn't at all reassuring.

The school was closed on Monday because the police were still searching the grounds for clues. We were stuck in the B&B while Mum waited to hear if the governors wanted her to go ahead with the project. We were watching an old black-and-white film on TV when DCI Swan paid us a visit.

The postmortem results had come through and they'd found tranquillizers in Mrs King's blood. Not enough to kill her, but enough to send her into a deep sleep.

"So someone did knock her out first!" I said to Graham.

"You're jumping to conclusions," DCI Swan told me, consulting her notebook. "I don't see any connection between the tranquillizers and her murder. You said in your statement you saw her taking tablets in the toilet?"

"She said she had a headache," I answered.

"It looks like she got the bottles muddled," DCI Swan told us. "She had sleeping pills as well as aspirin in her handbag. She simply picked out the wrong bottle – made a mistake and knocked herself out. And then Mr Walters made use of the tools at hand to kill her – the tools you had so conveniently provided."

"But our murder trail…" I protested limply, feeling stricken with guilt. "That was how the victim was supposed to die. Pills… Suffocation… And she really did. Doesn't that strike you as weird?"

"It certainly seems strangely coincidental," the policewoman conceded. "But you know, kids, sometimes things really are as straightforward as they appear. We'll continue our investigations, but I think you'll find we've got the right man in Mr Walters."

"But why was he even there?" I said. "Why would he kill her at a crowded event like that? Why not just hide down a dark alley and bash her over the head?"

"He says she phoned him, asking him to come in and discuss his son's behaviour. But there's no trace of such a call being made from the school office or indeed from Mrs King's phone."

"Hang on, though," I said, remembering. "I saw him answer his mobile. That's when he headed off towards the school."

"How do you know he was answering it? He could have been making a call," DCI Swan said coolly.

"I don't think so," I persisted. "He didn't press enough buttons. Although he could have been speed-dialling, I suppose."

The policewoman sighed wearily. "Rest assured we'll check his phone. If he received a call, we'll be able to trace who it was from."

She picked up her stuff and left.

I felt quite grumpy once she'd gone, and Graham didn't look any happier. When the film was over, we took ourselves off to the park to get some fresh air.

"I don't believe she muddled up her pills," I said crossly. We'd both met Mrs King – we'd had the full force of that personality blasted at us. And she wasn't just forceful: she was *efficient*. "I just can't see her making a mistake like that, can you?"

"Strictly speaking it's the kind of thing that could happen to anybody," replied Graham. "But to Mrs King? I'd have said the odds were against it."

"So what happened? Why would she have taken the wrong tablets?" I asked. An idea burst into my head like a firework. "Perhaps she took the right ones!"

"What do you mean?"

"It's easy enough to put the wrong tablets in the right bottle," I suggested.

"So she thought she was taking aspirin, but some-one had put sleeping pills in that particular bottle?" Graham looked at me and I nodded. I started to imagine how it could have happened.

"It would only have taken a couple of minutes. You'd have had to take the bottles out of her handbag and swap the contents around, then get them back in again."

"Maybe not even that," said Graham. "You could have prepared one earlier. Just swapped her aspirin bottle with the dodgy one."

"And then changed it back after she was dead."

Graham nodded. "And it would be logical to assume that whoever did it must also have suffocated her. That would have been an easy task if she was deeply asleep."

"So we should start by working out who could have got to her handbag that afternoon." I considered the subject. "She dumped it at the back of the hall at the start of the meeting, didn't she? Anyone could have got to it while she was doing her Winston Churchill bit – everyone was looking at her. And all the staff and half the parents were there."

"Not all the staff," said Graham. "Mrs Plumtree arrived late, remember?"

"True. And then she was stuck in the office looking

after Ricky. She couldn't even get out to take Mrs King her tea, could she? I guess she's off the hook. But practically the whole school and their entire families turned out for the fayre. Where was Mrs King's handbag when she did her opening speech?"

"She gave it to Mr Piper," said Graham.

"So she did. And then after I found Mrs King's body there was all that chaos and confusion with everyone running around... *Anyone* could have slipped *anything* in her bag *any time*." I looked at Graham.

"So what you're saying is that absolutely everyone is a suspect," he said gloomily.

"That's about it, yes. Including you and me, seeing as we planned the whole thing. I wonder how we're going to solve this one?"

theft

The next morning the pupils of St Andrew's returned to school. It was on the local news. They were supposed to "settle back into their normal routine" according to Mr Edwards, who stood by the gates, hale and hearty, shepherding staff and pupils through and keeping journalists at bay.

It didn't look very normal. For a start there were photographers lurking behind bushes trying to take pictures of the murder scene. The kids and parents all looked stunned, as if they didn't expect sudden death to happen to anyone they knew. But the police had arrested the right man, so Mr Edwards kept telling people as they came in, repeating it so often that it sounded like the rousing chorus to a jolly folk song.

Mum received a phone call at about 9.30 from Mr Piper, who was now acting head. He told her they'd raised £871.26 at the fayre and, combined with the money that was already in the school fund, there was enough to complete the environmental area. Could she come in with her plans?

Graham and I were keen to get another look at the crime scene, so we went along too. By 9.45 we were walking up the path towards the reception area.

But before we even set foot through the door I could feel things weren't right. The hairs on the back of my neck stood up as if a cold draught was blowing down my shirt.

Mrs Plumtree's window was closed, so Mum tapped on the glass. Looking through it, everything seemed to be the same. There was the collection of Davy-travels-the-world photographs next to her computer. There was Mrs Plumtree, fingers on her computer keyboard, staring at the screen. But that was what was wrong. She wasn't moving. Mum tapped again and it was a full five seconds before the secretary responded.

She turned slowly in her chair and raised herself awkwardly to her feet. Her face was a ghastly white, and as she came to the window to slide it open I could see her hands were shaking.

"Is something wrong?" asked Mum.

"I don't understand," Mrs Plumtree said in a voice quavering with distress. "It can't have. I don't believe it! It's impossible!" She made a noise in the back of her throat – kind of a cross between a whimper and a sob. "I don't understand!" she gasped. "No! No!"

"Mrs Plumtree?" Mum said. "Do you want me to do anything?"

"Yes, dear." The words fell out of the secretary's mouth as if they were choking her. I could see she felt too weak to stay standing. "Fetch Mr Piper."

"Go on, Poppy." Mum pushed me in the direction of the head's office while she fussed over Mrs Plumtree, persuading her to sit back down and take deep breaths.

Even though she was no longer there, Mrs King's office was still full of her presence, somehow. I half expected to hear her telling me off for going in without knocking. Instead, Mr Piper was in there, a strange half-smile on his face, leaning back in Mrs King's chair. It seemed too big for him – like he was a child sitting in a grown-up's place.

"Mrs Plumtree wants you," I said. "Something's happened."

He followed me without a word. As soon as she saw him, Mrs Plumtree burst out, "Someone's stolen the money! We had almost five thousand pounds in the school fund at the beginning of term. And now it's gone. All of it. Look!" She pointed at the computer with a trembling finger.

There was a deathly silence while Mr Piper examined the screen.

"How could that happen?" he said shakily. "I thought only the head was authorized to draw funds from that account."

"No... There are two signatories," whispered Mrs Plumtree.

"Who are they?" demanded Mr Piper.

"Mrs King was one. And – oh dear – how could he do such a thing?" Mrs Plumtree tried to steady herself. "The other is Mr Edwards."

the crooked
chairman

Mum dispatched me and Graham to the staff room to make Mrs Plumtree a cup of tea.

"So," I said as we waited for the kettle to boil. "Mr Edwards nicked the school fund. No wonder he wasn't keen on the environmental area. I mean, Mrs King was bound to find out about the missing money as soon as the project got started."

"Embezzlement," said Graham thoughtfully. "As you know, arguments about money or property – in other words, financial reasons – come fifth on the list of most common motives for murder."

"Do you reckon Mr Edwards might have done away with Mrs King?"

"I think we ought to consider it as a possibility," said Graham.

"I suppose he could have done it, couldn't he?" I felt quite excited all of a sudden. "I mean, he came down the slope right after Mr Walters had run away. He could have been there all along. He could have killed Mrs King, then gone back up to hide until someone found her."

"It's not inconceivable that he switched the pills too. He was there at the meeting, wasn't he?"

"Hey!" I grabbed Graham's arm. "Do you reckon he framed Mr Walters?"

"How do you mean?"

"Well, maybe it was him who called Mr Walters on his mobile. He could have pretended to be Mrs King."

"That's highly unlikely," said Graham. "Mr Walters would have known it was a man ringing him."

"Not if he disguised his voice," I persisted. "If he'd talked all high pitched and if the line was crackly or there was lots of background noise – and there was loads of that at the fayre, wasn't there? – he might have got away with it. He could have lured Mr Walters down there so he would get the blame."

"If your theory is correct – and personally I think it's stretching plausibility a tad too far – Mr Edwards must have set up the murder trail to get rid of Mrs King before she found out he'd stolen the school funds," said Graham slowly.

"In which case he's the sheepdog," I said, pouring boiling water onto a teabag and slopping in a bit of milk. "He was the one who was steering everything along."

"The open-and-shut case against Mr Walters seems to have developed faulty hinges," said Graham, pushing the sugar towards me. "I wonder what DCI Swan will say?"

DCI Swan didn't say much at all.

By the time we took Mrs Plumtree her tea, the policewoman was sitting in the office listening to the long and distressing tale of the vanished funds. Mrs Plumtree had taken the whole thing very personally: she was crying and emitting great gusts of floral perfume, and in between heaving sobs she kept saying, "It's all my fault! I should have noticed the money was missing before now. But I just didn't think to check. I only looked at it this morning so I could pay in what we made at the fayre. And now look what's happened! Mrs King dead! The money stolen! Oh dear! It's too awful."

I couldn't help myself. I blurted out, "Do you think there's a connection with Mrs King's death?" and then wished I hadn't.

DCI Swan fixed me with an icy stare. "No, I don't," she said. "Theft is one thing. Murder is quite another. And the circumstantial evidence against Mr Walters is overwhelming." Just then her mobile rang. She listened to the person on the other end, gave a couple of grunts and hung up.

"The money's been found," she announced.

"Oh, good heavens!" exclaimed Mrs Plumtree. "But where? How?"

"Mr Edwards wasn't very clever about hiding it. It's right there in his bank account. Time I had a chat with him, I think."

She didn't give us another glance, but stalked out of the school building and down the drive to where a panda car was waiting for her.

We saw on the local news later that day that Mr Edwards had been arrested for fraud.

spring flowers

There didn't seem much point in us staying after that. Mr Edwards' bank account had been frozen by the police, so the school wouldn't get its money back for a while. And if it couldn't pay Mum, she couldn't very well do the job. "Pack your stuff, you two," she told me and Graham. "We may as well go home. But I can't face a five-hour drive today. We'll leave in the morning."

Before that, though, Mum decided to call on Mrs Plumtree. "Poor woman," she said. "She was so upset this morning! And it's not like she hasn't got enough on her plate without all that. She's been so kind to us. I'd like to say a proper goodbye. Maybe we could drop some flowers round to her."

So that's what we did. Just before tea, we walked around to Mrs Plumtree's house with a massive bunch of daffodils. We banged with the knocker and rang the doorbell, but no one answered. We were standing there, wondering whether or not to leave the flowers on the doorstep, when a wrinkly old woman peered out of the neighbouring house.

"Are you looking for Joyce?" she asked in a wibbly-wobbly old-person voice.

We had no idea what Mrs Plumtree's first name was, but we knew we were at the right house, so Mum said, "Yes."

"She's out, dear," the old woman answered, adding rather unnecessarily, "I'm Pearl, her neighbour. She's gone shopping with Ricky. Won't be back for a while, I'm afraid."

"We were hoping to give her these," Mum said, waving the daffodils. "Could we leave them with you?"

Pearl nodded and all three of us stepped across the low wall dividing the front gardens so that Mum could hand the flowers over. Which turned out to be a big mistake. Because once she had us in her garden, we were trapped. Pearl started talking. And talking. And talking. There was no escape. The more Mum smiled politely and nodded, the more the old lady went on. If we'd had any sense we'd have run away, but Graham and I had been Properly Brought Up and Mum Didn't Do Such Things, so we all had to stand there dying of boredom.

She started off with the weather ("Wasn't much of a summer last year, was it? Not like 1976. That was one to remember. Let's hope we get better weather this year. I could use a bit of sun."), progressed to the State of the Country ("Youth of today. They don't know they're born. Soft. That's what they are. Soft.") and the National Health Service ("Service? That's a joke. It's not what I'd call service.") and ended up with her bunions (the details of which were so grotesque, I won't repeat them). We were just losing the will to live, when Mrs Plumtree's car pulled up.

With a sigh of relief, Mum removed the flowers from the old woman's grasp. "We can deliver them now. We won't keep you any longer."

Pearl hadn't finished with us, though. She looked at Ricky, sitting in the front seat with the window wound down and his face half out as if he'd been enjoying the breeze, and tutted mournfully. "He'll be twenty-one next month. I can hardly believe it! He was such a lovely little lad," she said. "So sweet natured. So quiet."

"Really?" said Mum. "Poppy said he was quite upset at the spring fayre."

"Yes… Well, he doesn't like crowds these days. It's a pity, they never used to bother him. He was an absolute sweetie, you know, when he was younger. One of life's innocents, if you know what I mean. Never a shred of nastiness or spite. Wouldn't hurt a fly. He was always locked in his own little world, of course. But he made it look like a *nice* place to be." She gave a wistful laugh. "Some days I wished I could join him there."

Mrs Plumtree and Ricky got out of the car. She looked pale, but she waved and smiled at us before opening the boot to get the shopping out. As she and Ricky started up the path, we edged back towards the wall. But before we could escape Pearl's clutches she said to Mum, "He must be missing his brother, I suppose. We hardly see Davy these days. He's always off somewhere or other. I don't know how Joyce affords it, really I don't. And what with her retiring soon. How's she going to manage, I wonder?" She sighed and then added, "Ricky changed the day Davy went travelling. Poor lad. He never seemed quite the same again."

I was looking at Pearl when I felt it. Something weird. Nasty. Like a stab wound: a knife between my ribs. Someone was staring at me. At us. And that person was thinking thoughts that were Pure Evil. For the second time since we'd been in Barnford, I could smell malice in the air.

I looked wildly around but couldn't see anyone new in the street. There were Mrs Plumtree and Ricky struggling with the shopping. There was the old lady, still rabbiting on about Nothing in Particular.

And then I noticed Mr Piper coming up the road pushing a double buggy containing two chocolate-smeared children and my stomach turned right over. He called a cheery "Hello!" and stopped for a chat. He didn't stay long because the kids started to wail. "Better get going," he said, smiling at Mrs Plumtree. "These monsters need to be fed." He rolled his eyes heavenwards and added, "No rest for the wicked!"

Before he was even out of earshot, Pearl said to Mum, "He's the acting head now. That must mean more money, mustn't it? I heard they've been struggling lately. His wife's scared they might even lose the house. Nice for him to have a bit extra, what with the kiddies. They live in the next street, you know. Such a lovely family."

He reached the corner – a dad with his two small kids heading home for tea – and it should have been a nice, cosy sight. But just before he disappeared, he looked back over his shoulder and I could see he'd heard every word. The look he darted at Pearl was one of naked fury and I was totally unnerved by it. I could feel something ugly and menacing lurking; it was almost as if evil was shimmering in the street like a heat haze.

"Come on," I said to Graham. "Let's go."

I jumped over the wall, closely followed by a mystified Graham. With Mum trailing behind, we hurried back in the direction of the B&B before Mrs Plumtree had even had a chance to thank Mum for the flowers.

the plot thickens

I didn't even try to explain the odd sensation I'd had outside Mrs Plumtree's, because I knew Graham liked to stick to Scientifically Proven Facts. Instead I said, "Mr Piper gave Pearl a really nasty look back there."

"I can't say I'm entirely surprised," he replied. "I gather grown-ups don't take kindly to having their financial affairs gossiped about. He must have been terribly embarrassed."

I didn't push it any further but changed the subject slightly. "Speaking of financial affairs... I don't get it about Mr Edwards. Surely anyone clever enough to dream up a plot this complicated isn't going to make a stupid mistake about money? If he did nick it, he wouldn't have shoved it into his own bank, would he?"

"I agree," said Graham. "That would be too obvious. The sensible thing would be to hide it in an offshore account. The whole thing is very puzzling."

We walked back to the B&B lost in our own thoughts. When we got there we found DCI Swan waiting for us.

"You're quite sure that Mr Edwards started doing the murder trail *before* you saw Mr Walters answer his phone?" she demanded.

"Oh, he did answer it, then, did he?" I said, a bit sarcastically. "He wasn't dialling out?"

DCI Swan frowned. "No," she admitted. "You were right about that particular detail. We checked the phone log and it seems that the call to Mr Walters was in fact made from Mr Edwards' phone."

I looked at Graham in a told-you-so sort of way. Mr Edwards had pretended to be Mrs King and lured Mr Walters to the spot to frame him for her murder. I was right!

Or was I? If I was honest with myself, I had to admit that Mr Edwards didn't look like he'd be capable of imitating the head's voice. Not convincingly, anyway. Perhaps the man had hidden talents. Or did he?

Fortunately I kept my mouth shut. If I'd spoken just

then I'd have looked a complete idiot, because what DCI Swan said next blew my theory right out of the water.

"Mr Edwards' phone is the same make and model as Mrs King's. I admit I was a little puzzled by it, but the explanation is quite simple. We believe she picked up the wrong one by accident and called Mr Walters to tell him that his son would be permanently excluded."

"So Mr Walters was telling the truth about her ringing him?" I asked.

"It seems so," agreed the policewoman. "But then – finding her asleep – the temptation to silence her proved too much for him. He smothered her on impulse. And before you start going on about possible connections between the two incidents, let me state quite categorically that there isn't one. They are two different cases entirely. Both quite simple. Both clear cut. To the professionals, at any rate."

So there we were again with another open-and-shut case, and another suspect folded up nice and neatly inside it.

But as DCI Swan left the B&B I could see from Graham's face that he didn't believe it any more than I did.

I couldn't let go of the idea. Neither could Graham. We were both one hundred per cent certain that someone had phoned Mr Walters to lure him to where the body lay, and it wasn't Mrs King. The more we talked, the more we convinced ourselves that Mr Walters and Mr Edwards had both been framed. By the end of the day we'd have bet our entire savings that:

a) they were innocent; and

b) they'd been set up as part of the same grand plan.

But how on earth were we ever going to work out what that plan was, or who was behind it?

I found it hard to get to sleep that night. We were supposed to be heading home the following morning, and the thought of leaving before we'd worked out what had really happened to Mrs King made me tense and uncomfortable. I slept badly and woke up early, the sun streaming in through the cheap curtains of my room. I couldn't stay in bed any longer, so I got up and opened them.

It was a nice spring morning: the brightness of the sun made all the newly emerging leaves look unnaturally green. I was tetchy and restless. What I needed was a bit of exercise. Pulling on some clothes, I tiptoed out and posted a note for Mum under her door.

Graham was already up and dressed, and when he

heard me on the landing he came out of his room to meet me.

"Fancy a walk?" I asked. He nodded, and silently we slipped out of the house.

We headed for the park. If we were going to be stuck in the car for five hours, it made sense to get some fresh air – that's what I'd written on the note to Mum, anyway. The streets were quiet at that time in the morning and we didn't want to disturb anyone, so we didn't talk much. Until we reached the park gates I think we were both absorbed with our own thoughts. I'd half expected the gates to be shut, but a team of gardeners was already there, digging manure into a border at the entrance.

It was a big park, with a huge lawn adjoining a football pitch. We meandered around the bandstand and along a shady avenue between two columns of tall trees towards the play area.

If the sun hadn't been quite so bright, we might have missed them. As we reached the end of the avenue, a ray of light slanted through the leaves, glinting off the golden frame of a pair of glasses that lay on the earth, their lenses cracked and broken.

I thought somebody had dropped them: one of the gardeners, maybe, or a visitor. But then I saw a handbag, gaping wide open, its contents scattered among the leaf mould as if it had been rifled through. Someone had been mugged, that much was obvious. I was just opening my mouth to tell Graham, when I saw something far worse.

A hand – its fingers old and wrinkled – extended towards us from under a bush as if it was begging for help.

I couldn't speak. I just pointed. And then I walked towards the body.

"Don't touch anything," Graham warned.

"I won't," I said, and the words came out as dry as dead leaves. "I just want to check whether they're alive." I pulled aside a branch and with a jolt of pure horror recognized the person whose dead eyes were staring back at me.

It was Pearl.

a murderous job

It's difficult to get your legs to work properly when you're suffering from shock. Graham stayed to guard the body while I tried to sprint over to the team of gardeners at the gate, but with my limbs feeling like lead it ended up as more of a dazed stagger.

They could see a mile off that something had happened. I was still more than fifty metres away when one of them dropped his shovel and walked quickly towards me, saying, "What's wrong, love?"

"An old lady's been mugged. Killed! Back there."

It didn't take long for the whole emergency-disaster-blue-flashing-light machine to swing into operation. Once the gardener had called the police, the park was closed and they began the investigation into another murder.

DCI Swan drove me and Graham back to the B&B and took our very brief statements while Mum sat there looking appalled. I didn't say a thing about that horrible feeling of lurking evil I'd had yesterday when I'd seen Mr Piper, or the funny look that he'd given Pearl. This time I was sticking to the facts, pure and simple – at least as far as the policewoman was concerned.

But I knew that Pearl's death was too much of a coincidence. The words she'd spoken as Mr Piper walked away down the road echoed through my brain. "He's the acting head now. That must mean more money, mustn't it? I heard they've been struggling lately. His wife's scared they might even lose the house. Nice for him to have a bit extra, what with the kiddies." And what had Graham said? Financial reasons come fifth on the list of most common motives for murder.

New possibilities started to bubble away in the back of my mind, but I couldn't talk to Graham about them. Not yet. Mum was determined to get away as quickly as possible and was bustling around making sure we'd packed everything. "The sooner we leave here, the better," she said.

But before we could go, we had to force ourselves

to eat the Monster Fry Up that Majorie had prepared as a farewell breakfast.

Graham and I were pretty quiet while we ate, which was more than could be said for Marjorie, who had heard our news with avid interest. "I don't know what the town's coming to," she tutted. "All this crime! You'll be glad to go home, won't you?"

Mum didn't answer – her mouth was full of sausage and baked beans – but she nodded fervently and Marjorie carried on chatting.

Twenty minutes later, when we were stuffed, Mum went off to shower and brush her teeth while Graham and I loaded our bags into the car. It felt strangely unsatisfying to be leaving: like we'd been out-manoeuvred by someone. But who?

"Mr Piper," I said as we stood on the pavement next to the car. "I reckon it's him."

Graham looked at me. "It could be, in theory," he agreed. "Particularly if he was worried about money. But what about the rest of the teaching staff? They'd all have a motive, wouldn't they? There was that article in the newspaper about Mrs King's plans to get rid of the inefficient ones. I believe people can be very aggressive when it comes to defending their livelihoods. We should go back to where this began and look thoroughly at each and every one of them."

"OK, let's start with the fayre," I said, trying to be Cool and Logical like Graham. "Most of the teachers stayed on the field that afternoon, didn't they? They were stuck on their stalls."

"Yes." Graham nodded.

I screwed my eyes tight shut, running the fayre behind the lids like a speeded-up film. "As far as I can remember, only three teachers left the field that afternoon. Mr Piper rushed to the supermarket for coconuts. Mr Stuart got changed. And Miss Maris made herself a cup of tea."

"Let's find out more about those three, then," said Graham. "I expect the school has its own website. Do you think we could have a look on your mother's laptop?"

"Yes. But we'd better be quick."

We went inside, unpacked the laptop and fired it up while Mum was still in the bathroom. In a couple of minutes, Graham had tracked down the St Andrew's School site, which included, as he'd suspected, staff profiles.

It turned out that Mr Piper's speciality was IT. Graham whistled through his teeth.

"So he knows about computers," he said. "That opens up all sorts of options."

"What do you mean?"

"He could have hacked into the school fund," mused Graham. "It would be a relatively easy task for an expert to transfer funds to Mr Edwards' account without him knowing."

"So you're saying Mr Piper could have framed Mr Edwards?" I asked.

Graham nodded. "But I don't know why he'd want to."

"Maybe Mr Edwards didn't like him. He might have wanted to stop Mr Piper from becoming acting head or something. So he had to be got out of the way." Suddenly I got all excited. "Mr Piper could have swapped Mrs King's pills, too – he was holding her bag when she did her opening speech. He went to the supermarket just before four o'clock, but he was back on the field a couple of minutes after you'd seen Mrs King yawning. The timing would be really tight, but he could have killed her. And the murder trail was his idea in the first place, wasn't it?"

"Was it?" Graham was frowning, putting the brakes on my enthusiasm. "I recall Mrs King telling us it was. But when we started planning it in the library, I seem to remember that Miss Maris told us Mr Stuart had thought it up."

My shoulders drooped. "Oh… Yes, I think she did." I sighed. "It's like a smokescreen, isn't it? All those different rumours about who said what to whom? Do you think we'll ever see through it?"

"We can but try," said Graham "Let's have a look at Mr Stuart." He clicked on the teacher's picture, and when a potted profile came up, he whistled through his teeth again. "Mr Stuart runs the after-school chess club. So he's a good strategist, capable of planning several moves ahead."

"You said that whoever was behind this had planned it like a chess game." I was feeling dead confused. "But does Mr Stuart have the killer instinct?"

"He seems a pleasant individual," replied Graham. "He must have a fairly good-natured temperament if he was prepared to have wet sponges thrown at him all afternoon. But maybe if his job was on the line..." He left the sentence unfinished.

"OK," I said. "Well, Mr Stuart went off but he was there on his stall again when I rushed to the loo. So he could have killed Mrs King too."

"But we mustn't forget the phone call to Mr Walters," Graham reminded me. "Someone lured him to where Mrs King's body lay. Could it have been Mr Stuart?"

I shut my eyes, picturing the scene. "No," I said at last. "He was there getting soaked when Mr Walters answered his phone. But Mr Piper could have done it.

Or – if we're looking at everyone – Miss Maris went for a cup of tea before Mr Walters took that call. Mr Edwards could easily have left his phone in the staff room. Maybe she did it."

"She'd only have had about two minutes."

"The same as Mr Piper."

"Who was collecting coconuts."

"Allegedly." I sighed, then banged my hand on the table in frustration. "But what about Mr Edwards? What about Pearl? Where do they fit in? This whole thing's like a maze. Someone's set up all these openings that lead into dead ends. How are we going to find our way through it?"

"We have to," Graham replied solidly. "Mrs King was murdered. So was Pearl. They both died at the hands of a person or persons unknown."

"Person or persons," I repeated. Suddenly a new thought hit me and a cold chill prickled down my spine. "There's something we haven't thought of," I said quietly. "Something far worse."

"What's that?"

"The teachers could be working together."

teamwork

We were already in the car, heading for the motor-way, when Mum's phone rang. She pulled over to answer it.

It had honestly never occurred to me that there might be a Mr King. Mrs King had been such a massive personality, that the concept of her sharing a house with another living, breathing human being seemed totally implausible.

But that very morning Mrs King's husband had materialized in the St Andrew's School assembly. He'd insisted on donating enough money for the environmental area to go ahead and had written out a cheque on the spot.

"My wife was very keen on the project," he'd explained tearfully to everyone. "She kept talking about it. It would be a fitting memorial to an extraordinary lady. Perhaps you could erect a plaque. Or something..." Then he'd turned, vanishing from the hall as rapidly as he'd appeared. Mr Piper had been left standing on the stage waving the flimsy piece of paper from side to side to dry the ink, looking absolutely astonished.

But at the end of assembly he'd got Mrs Plumtree to put a phone call through to Mum, asking her to bring her plans up to the school as soon as possible. So instead of driving us home, she steered the car back towards Barnford.

"It's odd, really," Mum said as we neared the school. "Making a memorial to someone who was so unpopular. It feels quite strange."

"Unpopular?" I echoed. It suddenly felt weird to hear Mrs King described in that way. Forceful? Yes. Bossy? Definitely. Overbearing? Absolutely. But I thought people had actually secretly admired her for it. It was the reason the governors had given her the job, wasn't it? To sort out a failing school? Didn't they need someone who didn't mind making a few enemies?

"Yes," Mum continued. "Mrs Plumtree said on the phone just now that most of the teachers hated her.

She was planning on sacking three of them. The letters were all typed and ready, but she died before she could sign them. Mr Piper was due for the chop. And yet here he is wanting me to start digging tomorrow."

"Did she mention which of the other teachers were going to go?" I asked Mum, attempting to sound casual.

"Yes. That nice Mr Stuart, and the librarian, Miss Maris."

I didn't ask anything else: my mind was working fast, trying to picture the three of them hatching a grand plan to save themselves by doing away with Mrs King. It was theoretically plausible, as Graham would say.

Mum made a left turn at the roundabout. "Will you two be OK looking after yourselves today? I don't like leaving you, really. I'll give the B&B a quick call and let Marjorie know we'll be staying on – you can go back there and read, can't you?"

Graham and I nodded and looked Trustworthy and Reliable.

"Right," said Mum, frowning anxiously. "Just don't go finding any more dead bodies if you can help it. Oh – and don't tell anyone what I just said about the teachers, will you? I don't suppose Mrs Plumtree meant to tell me all that. She was just stressed about her neighbour. It was such a dreadful thing to happen! Poor Mrs Plumtree. She'll be glad to retire, I should think."

Mum parked outside the school, grabbed her folder full of plans and headed up the drive towards reception. I watched her go, feeling a shiver of apprehension as Mr Piper came out to meet her, his hand clasping hers in a friendly greeting. Graham and I ambled in the other direction, towards the B&B. But as soon as we were safely out of sight, Graham pulled his mobile from his pocket and dialled the police station.

We were genuinely trying to be helpful, but the way DCI Swan treated us, you'd have thought we'd rung to suggest starting our very own Crime Campaign.

"All three teachers were there at the fayre," I explained carefully. "And all three of them could have done it, either on their own or working together."

"Motive?" snapped DCI Swan.

"Mrs King was going to sack them," I said. "And—"

"Do you think we're so stupid that we haven't looked into this?" the policewoman said, interrupting me before I could even mention Mr Piper. She didn't appear to require an answer, so I kept quiet. "And before you go accusing anyone else, let me tell you that we've looked at Mrs King's husband and her close friends and relatives. We've checked them all. We've arrested the right man, believe me."

"But Mrs Plumtree had typed up the letters!" I said bravely.

"Did she tell you that?"

"Er… No…" I said, because strictly speaking she hadn't told me, she'd told my mum – and I'd promised not to say anything.

"We've already been through the school computers," snarled DCI Swan. "There's no evidence whatsoever that the head was planning to lose any of her staff."

Graham – who'd had his ear pressed against the phone to listen in – now snatched it out of my hand. "They'll have wiped it!" he said eagerly. "Someone – maybe Mr Piper – had already hacked in and put the money in Mr Edwards' bank account. It would be easy to wipe letters from the system."

"You think someone hacked into the school computer?" DCI Swan's voice was quiet, but she sounded deadly – like a preying mantis about to strike.

Graham hadn't noticed. "I'm sure of it."

"You're wrong," she said firmly. "Mr Edwards wrote a cheque on the school fund chequebook. His signature was there in big, bold letters when he paid it into his own account."

"It could have been a forgery!" protested Graham.

"But it wasn't. There was nothing hi-tech about this. It was a simple, old-fashioned crime, just like the mugging. You've leapt to a false conclusion, kids. You're in that hamster wheel again, scurrying faster and faster and getting nowhere. You shouldn't let your imaginations run away with you."

She hung up and we deflated like punctured balloons. All our certainty, all our theories, shrivelled up until we both felt like little limp, damp pieces of rubber lying helpless on the floor.

foul language

We weren't the only ones feeling deflated that day.

We spent the morning reading and watching TV, but by lunchtime we were going stir-crazy. We decided we couldn't stand the B&B any longer, so we bought some sandwiches from the corner shop and took ourselves off to the park.

The avenue of trees was sealed off with scene-of-crime tape, but the playground at the far end was open. We walked across the football pitch and sat on the swings. We hadn't been there long when I noticed a boy standing beside the roundabout, listlessly spinning it first one way and then the other. Why wasn't he at school? I took a closer look.

"Isn't that Craig Walters?" I said.

"The boy who got excluded?" Graham peered at him. "Could be."

"Let's go and talk to him."

"Do we have to?" Graham protested. But when I jumped off the swing and set off across the playground, he followed.

Craig Walters looked *terrible*. I'd met his type before – we had plenty of kids like him in our school who thought it was wildly original to call my best mate "Gawky Graham" because he's terrible at sport, or "Geeky Graham" because he's good at computers. Craig was one of those boys who have a cocky swagger, a mocking grin and the sort of laugh that makes you feel hot and humiliated; he was a kid who'd bully anyone who showed the slightest sign of weakness. But all that noisy aggression had been wiped out of him by his dad's arrest. I guess that having a parent in custody can do that to a child.

When we approached him, his eyes seemed unnaturally big and he had a strange expression on his face. I was expecting to see bitterness, resentment, anger. I thought he might lash out at us.

But in fact he just looked lost. Confused. Worse than that: he looked scared. When Graham cleared his throat, Craig practically leapt out of his skin and then flinched as if he'd been hit.

"Is your name Craig?" I asked him.

I reckon the old Craig might have stuck his chin out and demanded, "What's it to you?" followed by a thump or a kick.

But the new Craig sank to the ground, covered his face with his hands and started to cry. He was talking, too. For a while I couldn't make out the words, but then he said, "I never did nothing. I never did!"

Graham tutted loudly enough for Craig to raise his head.

"I didn't swear. I didn't!" I realized he was talking about what had started it all – him being excluded from school for using bad language. He looked from Graham to me and his eyes were desperate. "You believe me, don't you?"

Graham put his hands on his hips and studied Craig. I didn't get a chance to answer, because Graham said, "Recent research shows that disruptive pupils like yourself frequently disown responsibility for their own actions. It's a characteristic pattern of behaviour."

Personally, I thought Graham was taking his life in his hands. I expected a fist to fly through the air and land on Graham's nose, but Craig didn't do a thing. Fresh tears leaked out of his eyes and he said sorrowfully, "But I didn't swear."

"Oh, really?" said Graham. He was looking as

though Craig had just assured him that the earth was flat or the moon was made of cream cheese.

"Nobody listens," wailed Craig. "No one believes me. But I didn't. Not this time. Honest."

He jumped up then, and ran off, and though I called after him he didn't turn back.

"Suppose he was telling the truth?" I asked Graham.

"That would seem to be highly improbable, given that he was on the verge of being permanently excluded," Graham said. "I think the chances that he was being sincere are very slim."

I wasn't so sure. "But why would he say it?"

"Perhaps he's in denial. It's a well-documented psychological phenomenon."

"OK." I shrugged. "But the last person you said was in denial was Craig's dad, and we both reckon he's innocent." I didn't push it because it was mostly true, what Graham said: Craig really was the bullying, lying type – it was clearly written all over him in big, block capitals. He practically had the word NASTY tattooed on his forehead. So why did I have the feeling that there was more to it? That Craig Walters might somehow be the key to the whole thing?

I didn't say any more about it, but it nagged away inside me like a stomachache. I kept thinking I was missing something. That if I could find just one extra piece, the confusing puzzle would fall into place. But it was worse than trying to grab a slippery bar of soap in a hot bath: I just couldn't get hold of it that day.

And by the time I did, my mum had reached the top of the murderer's To Kill list.

building site

The next morning, Mum was ready to start work on the environmental area. Graham and I didn't have anything better to do, so we volunteered our services as under-gardeners. I was really wound up, and although DCI Swan didn't believe us, I was still dead suspicious about the three teachers who'd been up for the sack. If Mum was going to be working near them with a load of pickaxes and other big, dangerous tools about, I wanted to be there to keep an eye on her. And them.

When we reached the school, Mr Piper came down the path to meet us. He'd just taken Mum's palm in both hands, when I had that horrible feeling of lurking evil again: it swept over me like a sudden frost.

I stared at Mr Piper. He was smiling at Mum, that was all. I looked around. Kids were starting to arrive. There was a stream of parents coming and going up the drive. A man in a helmet, fluorescent coat and protective mask was standing in the car park with a pneumatic drill, waiting to strip the tarmac off so Mum could start work. Everything looked fine, and yet my teeth were on edge as if someone was scraping away at a badly tuned violin.

"Goodness, he's here already," Mum said, looking at the workman. "I'd better get going. You two can wait in reception. I'll give you a shout when I need a hand."

Graham and I followed Mr Piper into the building. I didn't hear Mum greet the workman or give him directions about where to begin. I hardly registered the sound of the drill starting. But two seconds later, I heard her scream. It cut right through the noise of kids arriving and stuck in my chest like a spear. Before I knew it, I was running outside. Into the car park. To Mum.

By the time I reached her, she had stopped screaming. She was unconscious. Her silence was even more frightening. That, and all the blood.

Graham had followed me, tapping 999 into his phone as he ran. Mr Piper had appeared from nowhere and was on his knees, fingers pressed against Mum's arm, trying to stem the bleeding.

And me? I was completely useless. I just stood there, cold with fear, sick with shock, not even asking the workman what had happened. I had no idea whether Mr Piper was saving Mum's life or killing her; didn't know whether I should beat him off or help him. The sight of so much blood paralysed me and I couldn't speak.

Then I felt comforting arms around me, pressing me to a capacious bosom, and I was breathing in Mrs Plumtree's floral perfume as she said, "Don't worry, Poppy, your mum'll be fine. She'll be all right."

The ambulance came, and the paramedics put Mum on a stretcher and loaded her in. Graham and I squeezed in too, trying to keep out of the way while they attended to her.

In my weird numbed state I looked at the faces looking back at me. It was like staring at an old photograph. There was Mr Piper: shirt stained scarlet, eyes shocked and worried. Mrs Plumtree: oozing sympathy and concern. And the workman, his face still covered by the mask, his eyes... There was something about his eyes...

Then the door slammed shut and the siren screamed so loudly, it hit me like a fist to the chest, jerking my brain into working order.

As the ambulance pulled away, I realized I'd seen that workman somewhere before.

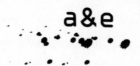

a&e

About five horrendously anxious minutes after we'd zoomed away from the school, Mum woke up enough to say, "Don't cry, Poppy. I'll be fine." Then she passed out again, and I must have made some sort of faint whimpering noise, because the paramedic said, "She's right, you know. Thank heavens that teacher got to her so quickly – he did a good job stopping the blood flow from her arm. She's not mortally wounded. It's a nasty cut but it's not going to kill her."

Just before we reached the hospital, Mum revived enough for me to ask, "What happened?"

"Oh, I don't know, really. What a stupid accident!

I was pointing out exactly where the workman should start drilling. I bent down just as he stepped forward, and caught my bum on his knee. Then I overbalanced and he got my arm with the edge of the drill."

"It could have been worse," said the paramedic.

"It could have been a lot worse," agreed Mum. "If I'd fallen the other way, it would have been my head under that drill, not my arm. I had a lucky escape."

The thought was enough to make me feel queasy.

When we got out of the ambulance, my knees had trouble holding me up, so it was just as well Graham and I had to do so much sitting around. We waited for Mum to go into X-ray and then be stitched and bandaged. By the time they'd finished, all the beds in the main ward were full, so Mum ended up in what they said was a disused office and Mum said was a broom cupboard.

"It's not very salubrious, I know," the nurse said. "But needs must. We're still going to keep you in for the night."

"But you can't," Mum protested weakly. "What about Poppy and Graham?"

"Don't worry," the nurse told her. "The hospital social worker will sort that out. You're going to need some pretty hefty painkillers; it's a nasty injury. You'll be in no fit state to look after them."

It turned out the nurse was right, because the minute she left the room, Mum started to doze off.

"That workman looked familiar," I said to Graham.

"Did he? I didn't notice."

We sat in silence for a while. I shut my eyes, trying to recall the workman's face. The first thing that floated into my head was an image of the Inca ruins of Machu Picchu. Weird, I thought. I opened my eyes, gave my head a little shake and tried again. This time the Eiffel Tower floated across the inside of my closed lids. Thinking that my brain had been affected by the shock of seeing Mum apparently lifeless on the tarmac, I tried again. Pyramids marched through my head like a train of camels.

For a moment I was tempted to give up. Then something stirred deep in the recesses of my memory. Photos. Snapshots on the wall. Exotic locations. A good-looking man smiling in all of them.

Davy.

Ricky's brother. Mrs Plumtree's other son.

That workman had the same brilliant blue eyes as Davy. Impossible! It couldn't really be him. Could it?

"He looked like Davy," I said to Graham.

"No! But he's in Peru, isn't he?"

"That's what I thought. There was that photo of him…"

Just then, Mum stirred and I said to her, as calmly as I could, "Where did the workman come from?"

"I don't know. Mrs Plumtree made the arrangements."

She fell asleep again.

"It can't have been Davy," I said to Graham. "Mrs Plumtree would have said something. I'm being stupid. I must have got it wrong."

Graham didn't answer. His face was showing signs of Deep Thought, so I just sat there and turned everything over in my head right from the beginning. I couldn't make sense of it. Nothing tied up.

Ricky. Brain-damaged since birth. Stayed at home while Davy travelled the world. But something snagged in my memory.

Pearl had liked him. Loved him, even. She'd come over all wistful when she'd been talking about Ricky. And the way she'd spoken – it was the way Mum talked about me in old photographs taken when I was small – as if the baby and the toddler in the pictures was lost for ever. It was almost as if the child the old lady had known had disappeared. Vanished. I remembered her exact words: "Ricky changed the day Davy went travelling." And then I'd had that weird feeling of lurking evil. I'd thought it was something to do with Mr Piper. Suppose I was wrong?

At last Graham spoke. "It was curious that the workman was wearing that kind of mask," he said thoughtfully. "They're normally used where there's asbestos. And there can't possibly have been any of that in the car park. Which *might* suggest he was wearing it to conceal his true identity."

"But Davy's in Peru. We saw the photograph."

Graham sighed. "Machu Picchu! I'd love to see the Inca ruins. They must be fascinating. They're unofficially rated as the eighth Wonder of the World. I keep trying to persuade my mother to take me to South America, but she says it's too expensive."

An echo of what Pearl had said drifted through my head. "He's always off somewhere or other. I don't know how Joyce affords it, really I don't." Mum had said something about the cost of those trips the very first day we went up to the school. But maybe Mrs Plumtree *couldn't* afford it. Suppose Davy hadn't really gone anywhere?

"Graham," I said slowly. "Could you fake photos like Davy's ones?"

"Easily." He shrugged, then went on for a bit about which computer programmes you'd use and how you'd alter the images. "But why would you want to?" he said.

Just then, Mum rolled over, focused on me, smiled

and looked at her bandaged arm. "I don't suppose I'll be able to dig for a while," she said. "This project does seem a bit doomed, doesn't it? I wonder if the environmental area will ever get started?" She took a sip of water and then her eyes closed again. She looked completely done in.

Whereas I felt like I might explode. In that one sentence, she'd handed over the final piece of the puzzle.

"The environmental area!" I gasped. "That's it!"

Graham blinked, startled by my sudden enthusiasm. "What?"

"It all started there, didn't it? The spring fayre was organized to raise money for it."

"I know that," he said. "I was present at that meeting, remember?"

"Yes, but we thought this whole plan was about killing Mrs King. We thought she'd made an enemy of whoever wanted to get rid of her. What if it wasn't personal?"

"How can murder not be personal?" Graham was baffled. "You can't get more personal than taking someone's life, can you? Why do it?"

"To stop the environmental area being built! Think about it, Graham. Mrs King comes up with the idea and she dies. Then Mr Piper says it's going ahead anyway, and the money goes missing. Then Mr King comes up with more money – and the day work is due to begin, it all stops because Mum has an accident! An accident with a dodgy workman, wearing an unnecessary mask, who looks like Davy Plumtree!"

"It makes sense," Graham acknowledged. "Sort of. But you'd have to be a fanatical anti-conservationist to object to a wildlife area."

"True," I agreed. "And I can't see why anyone would have it in for a bunch of butterflies. There must be something else…" I thought for a bit. "The car park," I said at last. "It's got to be something to do with the car park. The answer has to be there. Now, let's see. It was built two years ago."

"Two years ago," Graham mused. "When Davy went travelling."

"It keeps coming back to him and Ricky, doesn't it? And Ricky changed the day his brother left."

"He wasn't the same again," muttered Graham.

The words hung in the air while we both concentrated so hard you could hear the grinding of our brains.

But eventually I said tentatively, "Suppose he *really* wasn't the same? I mean *literally*. Suppose that's not him?"

"Who else could it be?" frowned Graham.

"They're twins, aren't they?"

"Well, yes," agreed Graham. "But no one could muddle them up. Ricky has special needs. It's obvious which one is which."

"What do you notice about Ricky?" I asked. "The fact that he's sweet and dreamy and always staring into space? If his hair was spiked up and he behaved differently, he'd be the dead spit of his brother." I was startled by the thought that occurred to me. "Could Davy be pretending to be Ricky?" It sounded stupid even to me.

Graham's mouth dropped open. "Why on earth would he want to do that?" he asked incredulously.

"No idea," I admitted. "But it fits. And Mrs Plumtree's neighbour died the day she told us how much Ricky had changed. If that *is* Davy, and he heard what she said, he must have thought she knew who he really was. Or he was scared she would work it out eventually."

"But Mrs Plumtree would know too," objected Graham. "Why would she agree to something like that?"

"Money," I replied. "You said yourself that it's fifth on the list of motives for murder. And Mum said something about her retiring early. So did her neighbour. Davy's twenty-one soon, isn't he? Suppose there's a rich relative around somewhere. Maybe there's some sort of will or something. Do you think they might be going to inherit some cash?"

"Mrs Plumtree…" Graham sighed. "She can't be involved in all of this: she was there in the office when Mrs King was murdered. We both heard her."

"We did. But hang on, Graham," I added as the seed of an idea began to sprout. "She was definitely in there, because everyone saw her – but was *he*? All we heard was someone crying. We assumed it was him. But maybe Mrs Plumtree was doing both voices and he wasn't in the office when we thought he was. They must be in on it together! It was a perfect alibi!"

"She made me take a cup of tea to Mrs King." Graham started to talk very fast. "Once I'd gone back to the field, he could have sneaked out and killed her. He'd have been safely in the office again by the time Mrs Plumtree handed you the biscuits. They could have been watching our every move from there. They'd have seen everything we did."

"Maybe Mrs Plumtree did all the other stuff too. Maybe Craig really didn't swear at her. If Mrs Plumtree told Mrs King he had, no one would believe Craig's word against hers. And yet it was a really good way of throwing suspicion onto Mr Walters. She could have made up that stuff about Mrs King wanting to sack the teachers too. Maybe it was her who started all those staff room stories about who wanted what and when for the murder trail. She's the sheepdog! It would only take a whisper here and there to get a rumour going."

"And the orange squash!" exclaimed Graham. "No wonder we had to run to the toilet so often. I suspect she put something in it so we had to keep going in and out of the building. We reinforced her alibi."

"She must have nicked Mr Edwards' phone and made the phone call to Mr Walters."

"And swapped Mrs King's pills while we were in the hall – she could have sneaked in at the back and done it before we noticed she'd arrived."

"I bet she got Mr Edwards to sign that cheque. He must have to sign things all the time, he probably didn't even look at what it was for. She did it all!"

We stared at each other, astounded. It worked. Each piece fitted. We were through the maze.

"But why would they want to stop the environmental area from being built?" asked Graham. "Has Mrs Plumtree got a phobia of invertebrates? Surely no one could be that scared of spiders?"

The realization hit me between the eyes like a sledgehammer. "It means tearing up the car park," I said flatly. "If that's really Davy, and he's impersonating his brother, it must mean Ricky's not around any more. What have they done with him, Graham?"

Graham paled. "You don't think...?"

I nodded, and swallowed hard before answering. "I do. And I reckon he's buried under the car park."

doctor death

Graham and I were so horrified about what we'd just worked out that we barely registered two medical staff entering the room. The doctor leant over Mum to examine her. The nurse stood to the side of me and Graham. Neither of us even looked up. It was only when I noticed a uniform out of the corner of my eye – stretched too tightly over an ample bosom – and caught a whiff of a familiar perfume that I reacted. Mrs Plumtree!

My instincts took over. My arm shot out and slapped the doctor's hand away from Mum. Which was just as well. He was holding a syringe, and I very much doubted that whatever was in there would make Mum better. It flew across the room and thudded into the wall like a dart.

Mrs Plumtree reached out for it, but Graham shoved the chair he'd been sitting on at her legs and she stumbled. He grabbed the syringe and pushed in the plunger so that the liquid – whatever it was – squirted harmlessly on the floor.

The two of us together could probably have defended ourselves against Mrs Plumtree. But when we looked at the doctor, we both panicked. It was Ricky. Hair spiked up, blue eyes sharply focused. Which meant it was really Davy, large as life and twice as lethal.

"Well, well, well," he said calmly, looking from me to Graham and back again. "My mother said you two were bright."

"Oh, they are," said Mrs Plumtree eagerly, blinking back the tears that had begun to well in the corners of her eyes. "It does seem a terrible pity. Are you quite sure you have to, dear?"

Davy looked at his mother, and she seemed to shrink a few centimetres. "Have I ever been wrong?"

"But they're *children*," she said in a whisper.

"Are you questioning my judgement?" Davy's voice was icy. "They'll tell the police. You don't want to see me in prison, do you?"

Mrs Plumtree hung her head. She said nothing, but her bosom heaved with emotion.

Davy took a step forward, fixing his cold, blue eyes on me. "I thought you might have worked it out. So I listened at the door. We heard your entire conversation. And now you have to die."

"Don't worry, dears." Mrs Plumtree's lower lip was wobbling as she spoke. "He won't hurt you. A few pills, that's all. It'll be just like going to sleep."

"But what will you do with our bodies?" Graham asked as if he was genuinely interested in the answer.

"We're in a hospital," said Davy, smiling a smile that chilled me to the core. "There's an incinerator in the basement. It'll take no time at all to dispose of you. And then I can live the life I deserve to. I've waited long enough for it."

"Why did you kill Ricky?" I demanded, staring at Mrs Plumtree and desperately trying to delay things.

Mrs Plumtree's mouth fell open, her head tipped back and for a few moments she looked as though she was letting out a silent scream. When she spoke, there was no doubting the pain in her words. "I didn't! He was my baby. How could you even think a mother could do such a thing?" Tears started to flow freely down her face and she made no attempt to wipe them away. "He had a weak heart, poor love. One night it just stopped. There was nothing I could do. I miss him so badly!"

"So what happened?" I turned to Davy. "Why did you start pretending to be him? Was it to do with money?"

"Well, of course it was to do with money," he said as if I'd asked the stupidest question in the world. "My wretched grandmother left everything to Ricky when she died. What did she expect me to do?"

Mrs Plumtree's voice was faint but she suddenly seemed determined to explain. "My mother was terribly fond of Ricky. She worried so much about what would happen to him when he grew up. He wasn't capable of looking after himself, you see. She left all her money in trust so that he could be properly cared for. Her will said that when he was twenty-one, Ricky would come into a small fortune. And if he died before then, it was to go to the local dogs' home. I don't understand why she did it. It was just so unfair on poor Davy."

Graham and I exchanged a swift glance and I knew he was thinking the same as me. Davy's grandmother had seen his true nature. It was a pity his mother wasn't quite so clear-sighted.

"She left you with no choice, didn't she, dear?" Mrs Plumtree continued. "When Ricky died, Davy told me exactly what had to be done."

"So you buried Ricky beneath the car park."

"Yes. The builders had cut right into the hill. There was a deep hole ready and waiting. It was good timing, really. So you can see why we had to stop Mrs King's project." She looked at her son proudly, as if they'd just announced in assembly how many house points he'd got that week. "Davy worked everything out. And it wasn't like he just had one idea – there were so many! Contingency plans, he called them, in case the first one failed."

"Contingency plans?" said Graham. "Like framing Mr Edwards? I suppose you made him sign a blank cheque weeks ago, didn't you, just in case it was required?"

Mrs Plumtree nodded.

"Is that why you spread those rumours about the teachers being sacked, too? And about Mr Piper struggling to keep his house? It was you who told Pearl that, wasn't it?" I asked.

"Well, yes, dear." She looked at us earnestly, pleading for our understanding and sympathy. "We have to get the project stopped. If Mr Piper still wants to go ahead, Davy plans to get him blamed for your mother's murder." Her eyes had grown wide and her voice shot up an octave. "I'm so lucky to have such a clever son! I did exactly what he told me to." She counted on her fingers as she spoke. "Suggested the trail. Steered it in the right direction. Got Mr Edwards to sign the cheque. Swapped the pills. Called Mr Walters." Her face clouded for a moment. "But I made a mistake, didn't I, dear?" She looked at Davy apologetically. "I used Mr Edwards' phone when I should have used Mrs King's. It confused the police for a while. But it all worked out in the end, didn't it?" She paused to draw breath and then said, "Poor Davy has had to live a double life for the past two years. But as soon as we have the money safely in the bank, all that will change." She beamed at her son, her eyes full of insanely desperate optimism that somehow – if she had enough faith in him – he'd make everything turn out all right.

"You killed Pearl, didn't you?" I asked Davy.

"Of course. She always liked a stroll in the park before sunset. It was the easiest thing in the world to fake a mugging. I really couldn't have her telling anyone else how much Ricky had changed." He smiled his chilling smile again. "But that's enough talking."

He looked at his mother. When he requested the bottle of pills, she handed them to him and watched while he carefully unscrewed the cap. But she dropped her eyes when Davy advanced towards us, and her tears splashed on the floor.

Graham and I were standing right by the bed. There were two of them and two of us. We probably could have put up an effective fight if Davy hadn't suddenly pulled the pillow out from beneath Mum's head and dangled it over her face. He held the pills in one hand, the pillow in the other.

"It wouldn't take much to finish her," he said calmly. "It would be as easy as killing Mrs King. A little messier than the injection I'd planned, but the end result will be the same. I suggest you take your medicine nicely, like good children."

I couldn't stand there and watch him suffocate Mum – I just couldn't. And though I knew that he'd kill her once he'd finished with us, I accepted the pills he shook out into my hand. So did Graham.

"Remember what DCI Swan said about us being hamsters?" I muttered to Graham.

"I do," he whispered, flashing one of his blink-and-you-miss-it grins.

We understood each other.

"Get on with it," said Davy menacingly.

We each put the first pill in our mouths. Swallowed. A second. Swallowed again. A third. A fourth. A fifth. I staggered a little and crossed my eyes.

"They're beginning to work," said Davy. "Mum, go and fetch a trolley. We can put them both on one of those and take them down to the incinerator. We'll finish the mother off later."

Mrs Plumtree stepped towards the door.

But before she could open it, the door was kicked open so violently that it came off its hinges, crashing into Mrs Plumtree and throwing her down hard on her back. Two armed police officers burst into the room, training their weapons on Davy and his flattened mother. And DCI Swan stood framed in the doorway, her mouth twisted into a reluctant smile.

For a moment I was impressed. I thought she'd worked it all out and sprung into action. But it turned out that Mum hadn't been quite as unconscious as she'd seemed. She'd come to when I'd smacked the syringe out of Davy's hand. Immobilized on the bed, she'd done the only thing she could before she passed out again – pressed DCI Swan's number on her mobile. The policewoman had heard the whole conversation and come straight away.

After Mrs Plumtree and her son were arrested, DCI Swan's hand landed on my shoulder. "We'd better get your stomachs pumped," she told me, and I couldn't help noticing that she seemed to find the prospect immensely cheering. "They'll have to shove a length of hosepipe down your throats to wash out all those pills. Unpleasant but necessary, I'm afraid."

"No need for that." I spat into my hand and held up the pills.

Graham did the same.

"We're not stupid," I said. "We stashed them in our cheeks and just pretended to swallow. Being like hamsters can be quite useful sometimes."

There's not much to add, really. Mr Walters and Mr Edwards both got released from custody immediately and without any charges, Craig was allowed back into school, and Mr Piper eventually got appointed as the new head teacher of St Andrew's.

When Davy's case finally came to court, he got the maximum sentence for the murders of Mrs King and Pearl and the attempted murders of me, Graham and Mum, not to mention the concealment of his brother's body and the framing of two innocent men. Mrs Plum-tree got pretty much the same, because even though she hadn't actually killed anyone, she'd helped Davy every step of the way.

When the car park got dug up, poor Ricky was given a proper burial at last.

The environmental area was brilliant when it was finally finished. It was based on Mum's design, although her arm was too mashed up for her to actually do it herself. The kids at St Andrew's worked on it together and it became a sort of memorial garden. We were invited to the official opening ceremony. There was a big plaque to commemorate Mrs King.

And an even bigger one for Ricky.

My name is Poppy Fields.
I never believed in ghosts –
until I stayed on a remote
Scottish island, and people
started dropping dead all
over the place. Was a spirit
taking revenge? When Graham
and I investigated, we began to
see right through it...

My name is Poppy Fields. I was
dead excited about my first trip
to America. But then people
started getting themselves killed
in really weird ways. Nothing
made sense until Graham and I
investigated, then the murders
seemed to tie together as neatly
as a string of sausages.
A little too neatly...

Stage Fright!

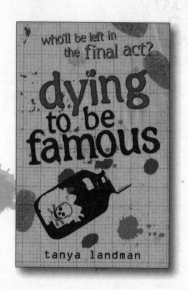

who'll be left in the final act?

dying to be famous

tanya landman

My name is Poppy Fields. When Graham
and I landed parts in a musical, we didn't
expect real drama. But then the star got
a death threat and the bodies started
stacking up. Before we knew it, we were at
the top of the murderer's list...